This book
belongs to

_____

_____

With love to Zoe Kennedy, Gbenga Chesterman,
William Evans and Alice Harvey who all got together
for a change at Suzannah and Lawrence's wedding -
and helped to make their wish come true

I.W.

For Jemma and Daniel with love

T.B.

First published in 2001 in Great Britain by Gullane Children's Books
This paperback edition published in 2002 by

GULLANE
CHILDREN'S BOOKS

Winchester House, 259-269 Old Marylebone Road,
London NW1 5XJ

1 3 5 7 9 10 8 6 4 2

Text © Ian Whybrow 2001
Illustrations © Tiphanie Beeke 2001

The right of Ian Whybrow and Tiphanie Beeke to be identified as the author and illustrator
of this work has been asserted by them in accordance with the Copyright, Designs, and Patents Act, 1988.

A CIP record for this title is available from the British Library.

ISBN 1-86233-385-8 hardback
ISBN 1-86233-374-2 paperback

Printed and bound in China

The Snow Friends

IAN WHYBROW
TIPHANIE BEEKE

GULLANE™
CHILDREN'S BOOKS

Not many small pigs like reading.
But Little Pig did.
He lived quietly on the edge of the wood,
under a big oak tree.

He had plenty of
acorns and twigs
and books, and for
a long time that
was enough for him.

Then, one day, he
found three new
words in a book.

Wish was one.
That was easy.

The next was harder.
It was **change**.

The last was hardest.
It was **friend**.

Little Pig closed
his eyes and tried
the words out.

"I **wish** for a **change**
and a **friend**," he
said to himself.

The **wish** worked. It started to snow.
And that was a nice **change**.

So Little Pig
took some acorns
and some twigs
and some snow.
And he made
a *friend*.
"Let's go," said
the snow friend.

And off they went,
until they came to an igloo.

It was the home of a lonely bird.
He was reading a book.

The bird said to Little Pig
and his snow friend,
"Tell me, do you
know these words?"

And he showed them *pig* and *together*.

"I am a **pig**," said Little Pig. "And my snow friend and I are **together**. What are you?" And the lonely bird told him he was a **penguin**.

"Which word do you like best?" Little Pig asked.
"**Book**, *wish*, *change*, *friend*,
pig, *penguin*, or **together**?"

"I like them all," said Penguin.
"But best of all, I like **together**.
That one lasts the longest."

"We like that
one best too,"
said Little Pig and
his snow friend,
together.

FRIENDS TOGETHER SHOP

IF YOU **WISH** FOR A **CHANGE**, GET **TOGETHER** HERE! READ A BOOK OR MAKE A NEW **FRIEND**!

Other Gullane Picture Books
for you to read:

Ordinary Audrey
PETER HARRIS • DAVID RUNERT

Harry and the Bucketful of Dinosaurs
IAN WHYBROW • ADRIAN REYNOLDS

Tabitha's Terrifically Tough Tooth
CHARLOTTE MIDDLETON

Over in the Meadow
JANE CABRERA

The Show at Rickety Barn
JEMMA BEEKE • LYNNE CHAPMAN

Old Mother Hubbard
JANE CABRERA

GULLANE
CHILDREN'S BOOKS